To the sweetest little girl
in California — with love from
Peggy Lee

9-6-38

AWAY RAN THE NAUGHTY LITTLE GINGERBREAD BOY

NURSERY TALES
CHILDREN LOVE

EDITED BY WATTY PIPER

PICTURES BY EULALIE

·NEW·YORK·
·THE·PLATT·&·MUNK·Cº INC·

CONTENTS

THE LITTLE RED HEN AND
THE GRAIN OF WHEAT

In a pretty little farmyard, once upon a time, lived a Little Red Hen and her brood of fluffy little chicks.

"Dear, oh dear," she sighed one day, "I must not forget that when winter comes the green meadows and fields will be cov-ered with snow. Then we cannot scratch for food. I must see that our little cupboard is filled with good things to eat before the cold weather sets in," and she bustled about her little house to make it neat and clean.

When the breakfast dishes

were washed and the beds made, she put on her pretty bonnet with the purple flower on it.

"Come, chicks," she clucked, as up the shady lane she hurried to the big farmyard.

"We must find some grains of wheat,
But the grains you must not eat."

"Why not?" asked her little chicks.

"Because when we the grains have found
We must sow them in the ground.
By and by they'll grow up tall
For the harvest in the Fall,"

answered the Little Red Hen,

While she hunted here and there,
Way, way yonder over there,
Till at last, with happy laugh,
She found some in a pile of chaff.

"Now who will help me sow the wheat?" asked the Little Red Hen, looking around at the barnyard folks as she hurried over to the garden with her apron full of grain.

"Not I," quacked the Duck.

"Not I," squeaked the Mouse.

"Not I," grunted the Pig.

"Dear me, what disagreeable people," thought the Weathercock on the Big Red Barn as he swung to and fro on his gilded toe, now south, now west as the wind thought best.

"Then I'll sow it myself," answered the Little Red Hen, and she scratched and scratched in the earth until she had made a nice little garden in which to plant the yellow seeds.

It was not an easy task to sow all the grains of wheat and cover them over with fresh earth, and the

Little Red Hen was very tired by sundown, but

The happy feeling in her heart
Told her she had done her part,

and gathering her little chicks, she led them home to the little house under the apple tree.

Soon the sunshine and the rain
Sprouted all the golden grain,
   And the wheat grew strong and
         tall
For the harvest in the Fall.

So one sunshiny day, the Little Red Hen started out by herself,

leaving her little chicks to play in the neat little house. Up the shady lane she hurried to the farmyard.

"Now who will help me cut the wheat?" she asked.

"Not I," quacked the Duck.

"Not I," squeaked the Mouse.

"Not I," grunted the Pig.

"Then I will cut it myself," said the Little Red Hen, and she bustled into the barn to find a sickle.

After that she set to work. And when it was all cut, it was time to go home to her little chicks, and down the shady lane she hurried to get supper for them.

Dear me, she was a tired little hen, but bright and early the next morning, she again hurried off to the Farmyard to thresh the wheat.

"Here she comes," thought the Weathercock on the big red barn, "I hope some kind person will help her this time," and whirling around on his gilded toe, he pointed the way the wind did blow.

"Cluck, cluck, cluckerty cluck,
It's time to thresh the wheat.
I must save each precious grain
While it's fresh and sweet.
Who will help me from the chaff
Every grain to beat?"

asked the Little Red Hen.

"Not I," quacked the Duck.
"Not I," squeaked the Mouse.
"Not I," grunted the Pig.

"Then I'll thresh it myself," answered the Little Red Hen, and with her smooth round stick, she beat the wheat from the stalks.

"There," she said, "now that's done," and gathering all the little grains in a big round pile, she asked: "Who will help me carry it to the windmill?"

"Not I," quacked the Duck.

"Not I," squeaked the Mouse.

"Not I," grunted the Pig.

"Then I'll carry it myself," answered the Little Red Hen, and bustling into the big red barn, she hunted around until she found an empty sack.

As soon as she had filled it with the grains of wheat, she placed it in a little wheelbarrow and set off down the road to the mill. There in the doorway stood the Rusty Dusty Miller, his hat and coat white with flour dust, while

Round and round went the mill's big sails,
Blown by the wind from the hill,

"WHO WILL HELP ME THRESH THE WHEAT?" ASKED
THE LITTLE RED HEN

Grinding the wheat into flour white
The farmer's sacks to fill.

"Good morning, Little Red Hen," said the Rusty Dusty Miller, politely taking off his dusty cap, "What have you in the sack?"

"Wheat which I have sown for bread,
Kind sir," the Little Red Hen said.

"Then I will grind it for you."

answered the Rusty Dusty Miller, and lifting the sack out of the little wheelbarrow, he carried it into the mill to grind it into nice white clean flour.

"Blow, good wind, until you find
There is nothing left to grind,"

sang the Rusty Dusty Miller.

Then filling the sack with the flour, he placed it in the wheelbarrow and home went the little hen singing merrily:

"Cluck, cluck, cluck, cluck,
I've sowed and reaped
  And threshed and gone to the
    mill.
I've carried this sack
  There and back,
Up and down the hill.
  And now I'll bake a loaf of bread
That we may have our fill."

  "Who will help me bake the bread," she asked on reaching the farmyard.
  "Not I," quacked the Duck.

"Not I," squeaked the Mouse.
"Not I," grunted the Pig.
"Then I'll bake it myself," answered the Little Red Hen, and she pushed the wheelbarrow down the shady lane until she came to her pretty house.

When it was baked, the Little Red Hen clucked happily:

  "The bread is baked
So light and sweet
  Now who will come
And help me EAT?"

"I will," quacked the Duck, waddling through the doorway.

"I will," squeaked the Mouse, peeking through a crack in the cupboard.

earned this bread for you, not for lazy folks."

"I will," grunted the Pig, looking through the window.

"No, you won't," answered the Little Red Hen. "I sowed the seeds, I reaped the wheat, I threshed the grain, I carried it to the mill and back again, I kneaded the dough and baked the bread. Cluck, cluck my little chicks. I

"Dear me," quacked the Duck, "why did I not help the Little Red Hen?"

"Oh! dear me," squeaked the Mouse, "I'm sorry I was so selfish."

"Dear me," grunted the Pig. "I was too lazy to help the Little Red Hen, so now I must go hungry."

"Eat it up, little chicks. Mother gives it all to you," clucked the Little Red Hen,

"Lazy folk must hungry go,
For they would not help me sow,
Neither would they help me reap,—
They had rather rest and sleep.

All alone I baked the bread,
Lazy
   Folk
      shall
         not
           be
         fed.

Eat it all, my chickies, do,—
Mother
     made
        it
          all
            for
              you.

THE TALE
OF PETER RABBIT

Once upon a time there were four little Rabbits, and their names were

Flopsy,

Mopsy,

Cotton-tail,

and Peter.

They lived with their Mother in a sand-bank, underneath the root of a very big fir-tree.

"Now, my dears," said old Mrs. Rabbit one morning, "you may go into the fields or down the lane, but

don't go into Mr. McGregor's garden: your Father had an accident there; he was put in a pie by Mrs. McGregor.

"Now run along, and don't get into mischief. I am going out."

Then old Mrs. Rabbit took a basket and her umbrella, and went through the wood to the baker's. She bought a loaf of brown bread and five currant buns.

Flopsy, Mopsy, and Cottontail, who were good little bunnies, went down the lane to gather blackberries;

But Peter, who was very naughty, ran straight away to Mr. McGregor's garden, and squeezed under the gate!

First he ate some lettuces and some French beans; and then he ate some radishes;

And then, feeling rather sick, he went to look for some parsley.

But round the end of a cucum-

up and ran after Peter, waving a rake and calling out, "Stop thief!"

Peter was most dreadfully frightened; he rushed all over the garden, for he had forgotten the way back to the gate.

He lost one of his shoes among

ber frame, whom should be meet but Mr. McGregor!

Mr. McGregor was on his hands and knees planting out young cabbages, but he jumped

the cabbages, and the other shoe amongst the potatoes.

After losing them, he ran on four legs and went faster, so that I think he might have got away altogether if he had not unfortunately run into a gooseberry net, and got caught by the large buttons on his jacket. It was a blue jacket with brass buttons, quite new.

Peter gave himself up for lost, and shed big tears; but his sobs were overheard by some friendly sparrows, who flew to him in great excitement, and implored him to exert himself.

Mr. McGregor came up with a sieve, which he intended to pop upon the top of Peter; but Peter wriggled out just in time, leaving his jacket behind him,

And rushed into the tool-shed, and jumped into a can. It would

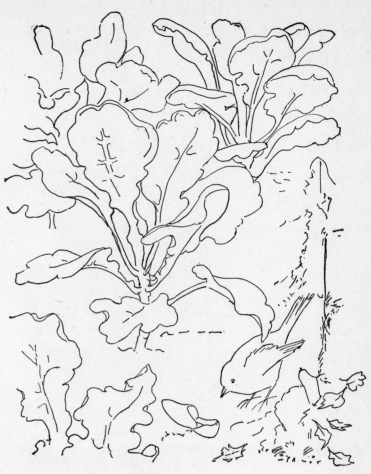

have been a beautiful thing to hide in, if it had not had so much water in it.

Mr. McGregor was quite sure that Peter was somewhere in the tool-shed, perhaps hidden underneath a flower-pot. He began to turn them over carefully, looking under each. Presently Peter sneezed — "Kertchoo!" Mr. McGregor was after him in no time,

And tried to put his foot upon Peter, who jumped out of a window, upsetting three plants. The

window was too small for Mr. McGregor, and he was tired of running after Peter. He went back to his work.

Peter sat down to rest; he was out of breath and trembling with fright, and he had not the least idea which way to go. Also he was very damp with sitting in that can.

After a time he began to wan-

He found a door in a wall; but it was locked, and there was no room for a fat little rabbit to squeeze underneath.

An old mouse was running in and out over the stone doorstep, carrying peas and beans to her family in the wood. Peter asked her the way to the gate, but she

der about, going lippity—lippity —not very fast, and looking all around.

had such a large pea in her mouth that she could not answer. She only shook her head at him. Peter began to cry.

Then he tried to find his way straight across the garden, but he became more and more puzzled. Presently, he came to a pond where

Mr. McGregor filled his water-cans. A white cat was staring at some gold-fish; she sat very, very still, but now and then the tip of her tail twitched as if it were alive. Peter thought it best to go away without speaking to her; he had heard

climbed upon a wheelbarrow, and peeped over. The first thing he saw was Mr. McGregor hoeing

about cats from his cousin, little Benjamin Bunny.

He went back towards the tool-shed, but suddenly, quite close to him, he heard the noise of a hoe— scr-r-ritch, scratch, scratch, scritch. Peter scuttered underneath the bushes. But presently, as nothing happened, he came out, and

onions. His back was turned towards Peter, and beyond him was the gate!

Peter got down very quietly off the wheelbarrow, and started running as fast as he could go along a straight walk behind some black-currant bushes.

Mr. McGregor caught sight of him at the corner, but Peter did not care. He slipped underneath the gate, and was safe at last in the wood outside the garden.

Mr. McGregor hung up the little jacket and the shoes for a scare-crow to frighten the blackbirds.

Peter never stopped running or looked behind him till he got home to the big fir-tree.

He was so tired that he flopped down upon the nice soft sand on the floor of the rabbit-hole, and shut his eyes.

His mother was busy cooking; she wondered what he had done with his clothes. It was the second little jacket and pair of shoes that Peter had lost in a fortnight!

I am sorry to say that Peter was not very well during the evening.

His mother put him to bed, and made some camomile tea; and she gave a dose of it to Peter!

"One tablespoonful to be taken at bed-time."

But Flopsy, Mopsy, and Cot-ton-tail had bread and milk and black-berries for supper.

THE THREE LITTLE PIGS

Once upon a time, long, long ago, there lived an old Mother Pig, who had three little pigs. Mother Pig was very poor and could not keep her children at home any longer, as it was a large task to keep and feed three growing boy piggies.

So one day with tears in her eyes, she said to each of them: "Little Piggies you are now growing quite big. You must go out and build your own little house to live in."

So the three little pigs started out to make their own way in the world.

They walked and walked, till they came to a big woods. And in the woods there were three roads. One little pig took the road to the right; one little pig took the road to the left; one little pig kept right straight on down the middle road.

The first little pig had not walked very far when he met a man carrying a bundle of straw.

"Please, Mr. Man," said the little Pig, "give me that straw, I want to make a house."

The man was good natured and felt sorry for the little Pig, so he gave him the straw and the little pig built his house.

The very next day, along came a big, bad wolf and knocked at the door.

"Hello, Little Pig!" he called, "Please let me come in, I want to speak to you."

"No, no, by the hair of my chinny, chin, chin, I won't let you in," said the little pig. "I hear you well from where you are."

Then the wolf growled: "Little Pig, you let me in, or I'll huff and I'll puff till I'll blow your house down."

But the little pig would not let him in.

So the wolf huffed and puffed, till he blew the house down and the little pig ran away.

The second little pig met a man with some wood.

"Please Mr. Man," said he, "give me that wood. I want to make a house."

The kind man gave him the wood and the little pig built his house.

When night came the little pig went to bed.

Soon, the big, bad wolf came along and rapped at the door, and the little pig got up and went to the window.

"Hello, Little Pig!" he called, "Let me come in."

"No, no, by the hair of my chinny, chin, chin, I won't let you in."

"Then," said the wolf, "I'll huff and I'll puff till I'll blow your house down."

Still the little pig would not let him in.

So the wolf huffed and puffed till he blew the house down and the little pig ran away so fast that the wolf could not catch him.

Now the third little pig walked along the road till he met a man with some bricks and mortar.

"Please Mr. Man," said he, "give me some bricks and mortar. I want to make a house."

The man gave him the bricks and mortar and the little pig built himself a nice strong little house with a green door, many large windows and a bright red roof.

The next day who should come along but the big, bad wolf. He looked all around the house to see who lived there. Presently he went up to the door and knocked.

The little pig looked out of the upstairs window and asked the wolf what he wanted.

"Hello, little pig," said the wolf, "let me come in."

"No, I will not let you in," said the pig. "Go away!"

"You had better let me in, Little Pig," said the wolf, "or I'll huff and I'll puff till I blow your house down."

"No, no, by the hair of my chinny, chin, chin, I won't let you in," replied the little pig.

So the wolf huffed and puffed, and puffed and huffed, but the strong little house would not come down. He took another big breath and huffed and puffed, but still he could not blow the house down.

When he found that all his huffing and puffing did no good, he tried to think of some other way to fool the little pig.

"Do you like turnips, Little Pig?" asked the wolf. "I know where there is a fine field full of them."

"Where, where?" asked the little pig.

"Why, down on Farmer Brown's field. Let us go and get some."

"What time do you go?" asked the little pig.

"I'll come for you at six o'clock tomorrow morning," answered the wolf.

"That's fine," said the little pig, "I'll be ready."

But he got up at five o'clock and was back home with a potful of turnips before the wolf got there.

When the wolf came at six o'clock and knocked at the door, the little pig called out, "why, I

"YOU MUST GO OUT AND BUILD YOUR OWN LITTLE HOUSE
TO LIVE IN," SAID MOTHER PIG.

have already found the field and I got some nice turnips for dinner."

Of course the wolf was very angry at this, and tried to think of another way to fool the little pig.

"Little Pig," said he, "I know where we can get some fine apples. Come with me tomorrow morning at five o'clock and I will show you."

"I'll be ready," said the little pig.

But he knew where the apples were too, down in Farmer Brown's orchard. He had seen them on his way home with the turnips. So the wise little pig went at four o'clock.

He was just climbing down from a tree, with a basketful of apples to take home, when who should come along but the big, bad wolf.

"Hello, Little Pig," said the wolf, "I see you got here before me."

My, but the little pig was dreadfully frightened.

"Are they sweet apples?" asked the wolf.

"But the little pig went before time as usual, and had a jolly time seeing the sights and riding on the merry-go-round.

He bought a big butter churn, and was just going to take it home when he saw the wolf coming up the hill. He had to hide quickly before the wolf saw him, so he got inside the churn, and in his hurry turned the churn on its side and it rolled down the hill with the little pig in it. Faster and faster and faster he went.

When the wolf looked up and saw this strange thing coming,

"Yes, very nice and sweet," said the little pig. "I'll throw one down to you." And he threw it as far from the tree as he could. The wolf ran to pick it up, and the little pig jumped down and ran home as fast as his little legs would go and locked the door behind him. So the big, bad wolf did not catch him that day.

The next day the wolf came again. "Little Pig," said he, "there is going to be a Fair in town today, don't you want to go?"

"Surely I will!" said the little pig. "What time will you be ready?"

"I'll be ready at three and we'll go together."

rolling, rolling, rolling, towards him, he was most dreadfully frightened. He didn't know what it was, but it looked like some kind of a monster. So he turned hurriedly in his tracks and ran as fast as his legs would carry him and for all we know, he is running still.

But the little pig got home safely and lived happy ever after.

THE COCK, THE MOUSE AND THE LITTLE RED HEN

A long time ago on a hillside stood a little white house with a green door and four green shutters, and in this little house lived A Cock and A Mouse and A Little Red Hen.

Across the valley on a hill stood another little house.

This little house was not well kept. The windows were broken, the doors creaked and the garden was full of weeds.

Now in this house lived A Wicked Fox and Four Bad Little Foxes.

One day the four little foxes came to their father,—"Oh father," they said, "we are so hungry, we have not eaten for three whole days."

The big fox sat thinking a long time, then in a gruff voice he said:

"Across the valley on the hill, there is a little house in which lives

A Cock, A Mouse and A Little Red Hen."

"And they are nice and fat," shouted the little foxes in glee!

"Fine," said the big fox, "I'll take my gunny sack and catch the Cock, the Mouse and the little Red Hen."

Then the four little foxes jumped for joy and said altogether:—

"We will prepare the fire for our dinner."

Away ran the big fox hiding behind rocks and bushes, until he reached the neat little white house.

Standing on tiptoes he peeked into the window, just as the Cock and the Mouse came grumbling down to the kitchen where the good little Red Hen like a bright Sunbeam was bustling about.

"Who'll bring in some wood to light the fire with?" she asked.

"I shan't," answered the Cock.

"Nor I," squeaked the lazy Mouse.

"Then I must do it myself," and to the woodpile she hurried.

"And now, who'll fill the kettle?" she asked.

"I shan't," answered the lazy Cock.

"Nor I," pouted the Mouse.

"Then I'll do it myself," answered the good little Red Hen, and off she hopped to the spring to fill the big iron kettle.

"Who'll cook the breakfast?" then asked the little Red Hen.

"I shan't," said the Cock.

"Nor I," squeaked the lazy Mouse.

"Then, I'll do it myself," said the good little Red Hen. And she did so at once.

All through the breakfast the Cock and the Mouse grumbled and grumbled, upsetting the milk and dropping crumbs on the floor.

"Who'll wash the dishes?"

asked the little Red Hen, hoping after breakfast they would not be so cross and grumpy.

"I shan't," answered the Cock.

"Nor I," pouted the Mouse.

"Then, I'll do it myself," said the good little Red Hen, and humming a little song, she soon had everything spic and span.

"Now, who'll help me make the beds?"

"I shan't," answered the Cock.

"Nor I," pouted the Mouse.

"Then I'll do it myself," and she tripped away upstairs.

But the lazy Cock and Mouse

looked about for a comfortable chair, and soon they were fast asleep.

As soon as the bad fox saw the Cock and the Mouse fast asleep, he knocked,—

Tap-tap-tap-tap on the door.

"I wonder who that can be?" said the sleepy mouse.

"Why don't you look," said the lazy cock.

"It must be the postman," said the mouse to himself, "and he may have a letter for me."

So without making sure who was there, he opened the door, and in jumped the big fox with a wicked smile upon his face.

"THEN I'LL DO IT MYSELF," SAID THE GOOD LITTLE
RED HEN.

But the fox with a cruel smile took the little Mouse by the tail and the Cock by the neck and tossed them into his gunny sack.

The little Red Hen hearing all the noise came running down stairs right into the arms of the sly fox, and he popped her into the bag with the Cock and the Mouse.

Out of his pocket he took a long piece of string and tightly

Screaming the little Mouse tried to hide in the cupboard. "Cock-a-Doodle," cried the Cock, as he jumped on the mantel very much frightened.

tied it around and around the mouth of the sack.

Then he put the sack on his back and down the hill he trudged.

As they were bumped about in the bag, the Cock and the Mouse were very sorry that they had been so cross and lazy.

They both began to cry and wonder what would happen to them.

"Cheer up," said the little Red Hen, "its never to late to mend. Look I have my work bag with me and soon you shall see what I am going to do."

By and by Mr. Fox was getting very tired from his heavy load and thought he would take a little nap and rest a while. So, when he came to a shady tree he dropped his sack and sat down beside it.

Soon he was fast asleep dreaming of what a fine dinner he and the four little greedy foxes would have when he reached home.

When the little Red Hen heard him snore, she opened her work

bag and took out a little pair of scissors, a needle and some thread and a little thimble.

But the fox heard her not and just kept snoring.

Quick as a wink, she cut a hole just large enough for the Mouse to creep through.

"Run," she whispered to the Mouse, "run as fast as you can and bring back a stone as large as you can."

And while the Mouse was dragging back the stone as big as himself, the little Red Hen snipped away at the hole until it was large enough for the Cock to get through.

"Run," she whispered to the Cock, "run as fast as you can and bring back a stone as large as you can."

The Cock soon came back with a stone as big as himself and they carefully pushed both stones into the sack.

Then the little Red Hen jumped out and brought a stone

as big as herself and also pushed it in the sack.

Taking out her needle and thread, she put on her thimble and sewed up the hole as quickly as she could.

Then all three ran for home, happy to get away from the bad fox.

They hurriedly shut and bolted the door, closed the windows and drew in the shutters and were glad to be safe home again.

"We will never be cross or grumble again," whispered the Cock and the Mouse to the good little Red Hen.

"We will light the fire and fill the kettle, we will get the breakfast and make the beds and you shall have a holiday and rest in the big arm chair by the window."

As for the bad old fox, he slept for a long, long time.

When he woke up, he rubbed his sleepy eyes and shouldered his sack, grumbling and saying, "I have overslept, and I must hurry home."

So the bad fox took a shorter

path home, that ran through the meadows, near a stream.

All of a sudden his foot slipped and off his back,—Splash,— dropped the sack into the water.

Quickly he tried to reach the sack but the stones were so heavy, that it quickly sank to the bottom.

"Dear, dear," he sighed, "there goes our dinner," and grumbling he went home to his four greedy little foxes who had to go to bed without any supper.

And to this day they never found out that the Cock, the Mouse and the little Red Hen are living happily together in the pretty little white house on the hillside.

PART TWO

AND LITTLE BLACK SAMBO SAID, "OH! PLEASE MR. TIGER, DON'T EAT ME UP."

THE STORY OF
LITTLE BLACK SAMBO

Once upon a time there was a little black boy, and his name was Little Black Sambo.

And his Mother was called Black Mumbo.

And his Father was called Black Jumbo.

And Black Mumbo made him a beautiful little Red Coat, and a pair of beautiful little Blue Trousers.

And Black Jumbo went to the Bazaar, and bought him a beautiful Green Umbrella, and a lovely little Pair of Purple Shoes with Crimson Soles and Crimson Linings.

And then wasn't Little Black Sambo grand?

So he put on all his Fine Clothes, and went out for a walk in the Jungle. And by and by he met a Tiger. And the Tiger said to him, "Little Black Sambo, I'm going to eat you up!"

And Little Black Sambo said,

"Oh! Please Mr. Tiger, don't eat me up, and I'll give you my beautiful little Red Coat."

So the Tiger said, "Very well, I won't eat you this time, but you must give me your beautiful little Red Coat." So the Tiger got poor Little Black Sambo's beautiful little Red Coat, and went away saying, "Now I'm the grandest Tiger in the Jungle."

And Little Black Sambo went on, and by and by he met another Tiger, and it said to him, "Little Black Sambo, I'm going to eat you up!"

And Little Black Sambo said,

"Oh! Please Mr. Tiger, don't eat me up, and I'll give you my beautiful little Blue Trousers."

So the Tiger said, "Very well, I won't eat you this time, but you must give me your beautiful little Blue Trousers." So the Tiger got poor Little Black Sambo's beautiful little Blue Trousers, and went away saying, "Now I'm the grandest Tiger in the Jungle."

And Little Black Sambo went on and by and by he met another Tiger, and it said to him, "Little Black Sambo, I'm going to eat you up!"

And Little Black Sambo said, "Oh! Please Mr. Tiger, don't eat me

up, and I'll give you my beautiful little Purple Shoes with Crimson Soles and Crimson Linings."

But the Tiger said, "What use would your shoes be to me? I've got four feet, and you've got only two; you haven't got enough shoes for me."

But Little Black Sambo said, "You could wear them on your ears."

"So I could," said the Tiger. "That's a very good idea. Give them to me, and I won't eat you this time."

So the Tiger got poor Little Black Sambo's beautiful little Purple Shoes with Crimson Soles and Crimson Linings, and went away saying, "Now I'm the grandest Tiger in the Jungle."

And by and by Little Black Sambo met another Tiger, and it said to him, "Little Black Sambo, I'm going to eat you up!"

And Little Black Sambo said, "Oh! Please Mr. Tiger, don't eat me up, and I'll give you my beautiful Green Umbrella."

But the Tiger said, "How can I carry an Umbrella, when I need all my paws for walking with?"

"You could tie a knot on your tail and carry it that way," said Little Black Sambo.

"So I could," said the Tiger. "Give it to me and I won't eat you this time." So he got poor Little Black Sambo's beautiful Green Umbrella, and went away saying, "Now I'm the grandest Tiger in the Jungle."

And poor Little Black Sambo went away crying, because the cruel Tigers had taken all his fine clothes.

Presently he heard a horrible noise that sounded like "Gr-r-r-rrrrrrr," and it got louder and louder. "Oh! dear!" said Little Black Sambo, "there are all the Tigers coming back to eat me up! What shall I do?" So he ran quickly to a palm-tree, and peeped round it to see what the matter was.

And there he saw all the Tigers fighting, and disputing which of them was the grandest. And at last they all got so angry that they jumped up and took off all the fine clothes, and began to

AND POOR LITTLE BLACK SAMBO WENT AWAY CRYING.

tear each other with their claws, and bite each other with their great big white teeth.

And they came, rolling and tumbling right to the foot of the very tree where Little Black Sambo was hiding, but he jumped quickly in behind another tree. And the Tigers all caught hold of each other's tails, as they wrangled and scrambled, and so they found themselves in a ring round the tree.

Then, when the Tigers were very wee and very far away, Little Black Sambo jumped up, and called out, "Oh! Tigers! why have you taken off all your nice clothes? Don't you want them any more?"

But the Tigers only answered, "Gr-r-rrrrr!"

Then Little Black Sambo said, "If you want them, say so, or I'll take them away."

But the Tigers would not let go each others' tails, and so they could only say "Gr-r-r-r-rrrrrrr!"

So Little Black Sambo put on all his fine clothes again and walked off.

And the Tigers were very, very angry, but still they would not let go of each others' tails. And they were so angry, that they ran round the tree, trying to eat each other up, and they ran faster and faster, till they were whirling round so fast that you couldn't see their legs at all.

And they still ran faster and faster, till they all just melted away, and there was nothing left but a great big pool of melted butter (or "ghi," as it is called in India) round the foot of the tree.

Now Black Jumbo was just coming home from his work, with

a great big brass pot in his arms, and when he saw what was left of all the tigers he said, "Oh! what lovely melted butter! I'll take that home to Black Mumbo for her to cook with."

So he put it all into the great big brass pot, and took it home to Black Mumbo to cook with.

When Black Mumbo saw the melted butter, wasn't she pleased! "Now," said she, "we'll all have pancakes for supper!"

So she got flour and eggs and milk and sugar and butter, and she made a huge big plate of most lovely pancakes. And she fried them in the melted butter which the Tigers had made, and they were just as yellow and brown as little Tigers.

And then they all sat down to supper. And Black Mumbo ate Twenty-seven pancakes, and Black Jumbo ate Fifty-five, but Little Black Sambo ate a Hundred and Sixty-nine, because he was so hungry.

THE GINGERBREAD BOY

Once upon a time, not so very long ago, there lived in a tiny house a little old woman and a little old man. They were very lonely, for they had no children of their own to fill their home with laughter and happy songs.

One day as the little old woman was baking gingerbread she said out loud, just to herself, you know, for her little old man was out in the garden, "I will make a gingerbread boy." So she mixed the gingerbread dough and rolled it out with care. Then with a round cooky cutter, she cut out a head and with her clever fingers, shaped the dough into a little round body, with a pair of arms and two sturdy legs.

"And now for the clothes," she laughed, and, pouring over

the gingerbread dough some hot chocolate syrup, she smoothed it into a nice little jacket and pair of trousers. With six fat raisins she made pretty buttons for his coat, and with pink sugar frosting she fashioned a little mouth. For his eyes she used two drops of sugar frosting and for his nose a tiny lump.

But how she knew that this gingerbread dough, when nicely baked, would hop out of the oven, I never can tell,—unless perhaps a pretty fairy had whispered in her dreams that such a wonderful thing would happen.

Then laying him on his back in the pan, she placed him in the oven and closed the door. And while she swept and cleaned the house, waiting for the little ginger-bread boy to grow glossy brown, the little canary bird sang from her gilded cage:

"Fire burn and oven bake,
Turn the little ginger cake
Waiting in the shiny pan
To a little ginger man."

The next moment the little old woman knew that her dream had come true when a little voice from the oven shouted:

"Open the door, open the door, I want to come out and play on the floor."

Dropping her broom, the happy little old woman ran to open the oven door and out jumped the gingerbread boy to the floor.

His chocloate jacket fitted so well,
If a tailor had made it you hardly could tell.
His eyes shone like stars, for the frosting of white
Had stolen a gleam from the warm firelight,
And the smile of the little pink mouth made him seem
To the little old woman the child of her dream.

AWAY RAN THE M

But, oh dear me! Instead of playing about in the neat little kitchen, away ran the naughty little gingerbread boy through the open door and into the yard, shouting at the top of his voice:

"A Gingerbread Boy, I am, I am;
I can run from you, I can, I can!"

"Stop, stop!" shouted the little old man in the garden, dropping his hoe, but the Gingerbread Boy paid no heed, and slipping through the gate, ran down the road as fast as his gingerbread legs would go, shouting at the top of his voice:

"A Gingerbread Boy, I am, I
    am;
I can run from you, I can, I
    can!"

By and by he came to a field
where the men were mowing the
tall waving grass with their long
scythes. Dear me, how the grass-
hoppers jumped here and there
for fear of losing one of their long
legs, and the little meadow mice
scampered about looking for new
homes.

"Stop, stop!" shouted the mowers on seeing the little Gingerbread
Boy, but he only answered:

"A Gingerbread Boy I am, I
    am;
I can run from you I can, I
    can!
I ran away from a little old
    woman,
A little old man,
And now from you I can run,
    I can!"

A little old man,
A field full of mowers,
And now from you I can run,
I can!"

and away he sped faster than ever, never heeding their cries of "Stop, stop, little Gingerbread Boy!"

After a while he met a Red Cow with soft brown eyes.

"Stop, stop!" she called, with a motherly laugh, "I'll take you home to my spotted calf."

"Not unless you catch me," he boasted, and down the lane he ran,

By and by he came to a big red barn by the side of a hill. Looking in through the open door he saw the farmers thrashing the wheat. "You can't catch me," he shouted, pausing for a moment in the doorway. Then away he ran, looking back and crying:

"A Gingerbread Boy I am, I
    am,
I can run from you I can, I
    can;
I ran away from a little old
    woman,

almost bumping into a big fat pig,
with a little curly tail, looking
through the old fence rail.

    "Stop and play with me a
       while,"
Cried the fat Pig with a smile.
But the little ginger boy
Answered, "Catch me if you
       can!"

and running down the lane, shouted back;

    "A Gingerbread Boy I am, I
       am,
    I can run from you, I can, I
       can;
    I ran away from a little old
       woman,
    A little old man,

A field full of mowers,
A barn full of thrashers,
An old red cow,
And now from you I can run,
   I can."

So on and on he ran until at last he came to the end of the road.

Then he turned up a path through the shady wood,

Where close to a brook a little house stood.
But the Gingerbread Boy never knew that within
Lived a wildcat with sharp claws and a terrible grin.
"Come in and have supper with me," said the sly old wildcat with a soft purr, opening the door as the tired little Gingerbread Boy sat down on the front step.

"Don't go in," whispered a little bird in the treetop, "that sly old wildcat will eat you for supper."

"Come in, come in," again purred the sly wildcat, who was too deaf to hear the little bird.

"Run home, run home before it is too late!" whispered the little bird from the treetop. "The little old woman with tears in her eyes is standing in the doorway waiting for you. Run home, run home before it is too late!"

"Don't keep me waiting," cried the Wildcat, and growing impatient, she stretched out her paws with their terrible claws.

"Run, run!" shouted the little bird, and with a frightened cry the little Gingerbread Boy turned and ran swiftly down the path through the woods to the roadway.

"Botheration!" snarled the sly wild cat as she turned back into her little house,

"The Gingerbread Boy smelt
        ever so nice,
I would like to lick the choco-
        late ice.
His candy eyes, so round and
        sweet,
And his buttons of raisins I'd
        like to eat."

On and on ran the little Gingerbread Boy; past the big fat Pig who grunted kindly, "Hurry hurry, hurry home!"

Past the motherly Red Cow, who softly mooed, "Hurry, hurry, hurry home!"

Past the barn full of thrashers, who smiled and shouted, "Hurry, hurry, hurry, home!"

Past the field where the mowers stopped their work to call out, "Hurry, hurry, hurry home!"

Past the little old man and right into the arms of the little old woman who pressed him to her heart and whispered, "Home again, my little Gingerbread Boy."

CHICKEN LITTLE

Once upon a time there lived in a tiny house with a pebbly roof and little red chimney, a dear little chicken named Chicken Little.

One morning as she was scratching in her garden a pebble fell off the roof and hit her on the head.

"Oh, dear me!" she cried, "the sky is falling. I must go and tell the king," and away she ran down the road.

By and by she met Henny Penny, with a basket of eggs under her wing on the way to the store.

"Where are you going?" asked Henny Penny.

"Oh, I'm going to tell the king the sky is falling," answered Chicken Little.

"How do you know the sky is falling?" asked Henny Penny.

"Because a piece of it fell on my head," she replied.

"May I come with you?" begged Henny Penny.

"Certainly," answered Chicken Little, and opening her little pink parasol, for the sun was hot, she hastened on, followed by Henny Penny. But a dusty road is no place for pretty feather dresses, and turning up a shady lane they met Cocky Locky.

"Cock-a-doodle-do,
The sky is lovely blue,"
he crowed.

"Don't be too sure," answered Henny Penny.

"Where are you two going?" asked Cocky Locky.

"Oh, we are going to tell the king the sky is falling," answered Henny Penny.

"How do you know?"

"Chicken Little told me," said Henny Penny.

"A piece of it fell on my head," cried Chicken Little.

"Cock - a - doodle - do! May I come with you too?" asked Cocky Locky.

"Certainly," answered Chicken Little.

Then away went the three, Chicken Little, Henny Penny and Cocky Locky along the Shady Lane where overhead the apple blossoms swayed in the merry breezes.

By and by they came to a pond where they met Ducky Daddles.

"Where are you three going?" he asked, paddling up to the bank so he could hear better.

"The sky is falling and we are going to tell the king," answered Cocky Locky.

"How do you know?" asked Ducky Daddles.

"Henny Penny told me," said Cocky Locky;

"Chicken Little told me," said Henny Penny;

"A piece of it fell on my head," cried Chicken Little.

"May I come with you?" asked Ducky Daddles.

"Certainly," they answered.

So they went along, but not so very fast because Ducky Daddles was pokey slow on his feet, although he could swim very well.

By and by whom should they meet but Goosey Poosey carrying a basket of gooseberries to market.

"Where are you four going?" she asked.

"The sky is falling and we are going to tell the king," answered Ducky Daddles.

"How do you know it is falling?"

"Cocky Locky told me," answered Ducky Daddles.

OUT FROM BEHIND THE ROCKS JUMPED FOXY LOXY

"Henny Penny told me," said Cocky Locky.

"Chicken Little told me," said Henny Penny.

"A piece of it fell on my head," cried Chicken Little.

"May I come with you?" asked Goosey Poosey.

"Certainly," said Chicken Little.

Then tightening the strings on her blue sunbonnet, Goosey Poosey followed Chicken Little, Henny Penny, Cocky Locky, and Ducky Daddles until they met Turkey Lurkey strutting around the old barnyard.

"Where are you five going?" asked Turkey Lurkey.

"The sky is falling and we're going to tell the king," answered Goosey Poosey.

"How do you know?" asked Turkey Lurkey.

"Ducky Daddles told me so," answered Goosey Poosey.

"Cocky Locky told me," answered Ducky Daddles.

"Henny Penny told me," said Cocky Locky.

"Chicken Little told me," said Henny Penny.

"A piece of it fell on my head," cried Chicken Little.

"If the sky is falling down,
It might hurt the King's gold crown,"

said Turkey Lurkey, spreading his tail out like a big feather fan. "May I come with you?"

"Certainly," said Chicken Little, Henny Penny, Cocky Locky, Ducky Daddles and Goosey Poosey.

So away they went until they came to a marshy meadow when all of a sudden they heard a loud hissing noise. There stood Gander Pander by a pool of water from which he had just gobbled up a little fish.

Where are you six going?" he asked, straightening his little black hat which had almost fallen into the water.

"The sky is falling and we are going to tell the King."

"How do you know?" asked Gander Pander.

"Goosey Poosey told me," said Turkey Lurkey.

"Ducky Daddles told me," said Goosey Poosey.

"Cocky Locky told me," said Ducky Daddles.

"Henny Penny told me," said Cocky Locky.

"Chicken Little told me," said Henny Penny

"A piece of it fell on my head," cried Chicken Little.

"May I come with you?" asked Gander Pander, wiping his feet on the grass.

"Certainly," answered all the little feathered folk.

So down a sunny path they went
To one another calling;
"We must hasten to the King
To say the sky is falling."

By and by they came to a wild, rocky place where there were only little patches of grass here and there and clumps of bushes. The ground was so rough and stony that they stopped to rest, when out from behind the rocks jumped Foxy Loxy.

"Where are you all going?" he asked, with a sly grin.

"The sky is falling and we are going to tell the King."

"How do you know?" asked Foxy Loxy squinting his eyes.

"Turkey Lurkey told me," said Gander Pander.

"Goosey Poosey told me," said Turkey Lurkey.

"Ducky Daddles told me," said Goosey Poosey.

"Cocky Locky told me," said Ducky Daddles.

"Henny Penny told me," said Cocky Locky.

"Chicken Little told me," said Henny Penny.

"A piece of it fell on my head," cried Chicken Little, "and we are going to tell the King."

"How silly!" thought wise Foxy

Loxy. "Whoever heard of the sky falling," but out loud he said, "you are not going the right way. Shall I show it to you?"

"Oh, certainly," they all answered and they followed Foxy Loxy up the stony path through the rocks and the bushes up the side of the hill until they came to a narrow dark hole, the door of Foxy Loxy's cave in the rocks. But of course, the trusting little feathered people didn't know that.

"This is a short way to the King's Palace; you'll soon get there if you follow me. I will go in first," said Foxy Loxy.

Just as the little feathered folk crowded around the dark narrow hole, eager to follow the sly fox, a little gray squirrel, with very bright eyes, jumped out from the bushes and whispered:

"Don't go in, don't go in,
See the fox's cruel grin
All your little necks he'll wring,
And you'll never see the King."

But the sharp ears of Foxy Loxy heard the warning, and, quick as a wink, he turned and caught Gander Pander.

Just as he was about to twist Gander Pander's neck the little

squirrel threw a big stone and hit the old fox right on the head.

"The sky surely is falling," groaned Foxy Loxy, creeping into the darkest corner of his cave.

"I'll lead the way to the King's palace; follow me," shouted the little squirrel.

Happy to escape from the wicked old fox, away ran Chicken Little, Henny Penny, Cocky Locky, Ducky Daddles, Goosey Poosey, Turkey Lurkey and Gander Pander.

By and by they came to the

beautiful palace in which lived the wise King, and following the little squirrel into the throne room, they all shouted at once; "Good and wise King, we have come to warn you that the sky is falling!"

"How do you know the sky is falling, my good subjects?" asked the King.

"Because a piece of it fell on my head," said Chicken Little.

"Come nearer, Chicken Little," said the King and leaning from his velvet throne, he picked the pebble from the feathers of Chicken Little's head.

"You see it was only a little pebble and not part of the sky at all," said the King.

"Go home in peace and do not fear because the sky cannot fall; only rain falls from the sky."

Weary but wiser, the little feathered folk left the palace and started on their long journey homeward.

"I guess the King is right," sighed Henny Penny.

"He certainly is," said Cocky Locky.

"I think so, too," quacked Ducky Daddles.

"I'm sure he is," cried Goosey Poosey.

And so said Turkey Lurkey and Gander Pander.

THE THREE LITTLE KITTENS

Once upon a time there were three little kittens and their names were Brownie, Blackie and Snow-ball.

They lived with their mother in a pretty little cottage near Farmer Brown's meadow.

All day long they would play happily together, never being cross with each other and always sharing their toys and playthings.

One day Mamma Cat gave each of them a nice new pair of mittens.

Brownie's mittens were a beautiful red color.

Oh! but they had a glorious time playing hide and seek, skipping rope and chasing the little field mice.

After a time their little paws became very warm and they took off the new mittens and put them down in the field.

In a little while Mamma Cat called, "Come Brownie, Blackie and Snowball. Dinner is ready."

So the three little kittens ran home hurriedly, but alas, when they got there Mamma Cat found that—

Blackie's mittens were a lovely green color.

And Snowball's mittens were bright blue.

My, but they were three happy little kittens.

Mamma Cat said, "Now, kittens, you may go out in the meadow and play, but be careful you do not lose your mittens."

So away ran Brownie, Blackie and Snowball, as fast as their little legs could go.

The three little kittens, they lost
    their mittens,
And they began to cry,
"Oh! Mammy dear, we sadly fear,
Our mittens we have lost!"

"What! Lost your mittens, you
    naughty kittens!
Then you shall have no pie."
Miew, miew, miew, miew.

"Now," said Mamma Cat, "run
straight away where you were
playing and find your mittens."
Away scampered the three little kittens, and sure enough, right
where they had left them—

The three little kittens, they found
    their mittens,
And they began to cry,
"Oh! Mammy dear, see here, see
    here,
Our mittens we have found!"

"What found your mittens, you
    darling kittens!
Then you shall have some pie."
Purr, purr, purr, purr.

"Now put on your mittens,"
said Mamma Cat, "and come and
eat your pie."

Now go right away and wash your mittens."

The three little k i t t e n s, they washed their mittens,
And hung them up to dry;
"Oh! Mammy dear, look here, look here!
Our mittens we have washed!"

"What! washed your mittens, you darling kittens!—
But I smell a rat close by!"
Hush! Hush! miew, miew,
Miew, miew, miew, miew.

The three little kittens put on their mittens
And soon ate up the pie.
"Oh! Mammy dear, we greatly fear
Our mittens we have soiled."

"What! soiled your mittens, you naughty kittens!"
Then they began to sigh.
Miew, miew, miew, miew.

Then Mamma Cat said to her three little kittens, "It is v e r y naughty to lose or soil your clothes.